To my little Johanna.

G. E.

For Iris and Luna, born on a winter day in the Southern light...

F. K.

© for the French edition: L'Élan vert, Saint-Pierre-des-Corps, 2016
Title of the original edition: Anna et Johanna
© for the English edition: Prestel Verlag, Munich • London • New York, 2018
A member of Verlagsgruppe Random House GmbH
Neumarkter Strasse 28 • 81673 Munich

Prestel Publishing Ltd.
14-17 Wells Street
London W1T 3PD

Prestel Publishing
900 Broadway, Suite 603
New York, NY 10003

Library of Congress Control Number: 2017953132
A CIP catalogue record for this book is available from the British Library.

Translated from the French by Paul Kelly
Copyediting: Brad Finger
Project management: Melanie Schöni
Production management: Astrid Wedemeyer
Typesetting: textum GmbH, München
Printing and binding: TBB, a.s.
Paper: Condat matt Périgord

FSC® MIX From responsible sources FSC® C022120

Verlagsgruppe Random House FSC® N001967

Printed in Slovakia

ISBN 978-3-7913-7345-4
www.prestel.com

GÉRALDINE ELSCHNER

and Johanna Anna

FLORENCE KŒNIG

Prestel

Munich · London · New York

Delft, October 12th, 1666

Hippity hop! From left to right and right to left, the spindles bob up and down on Anna's cushion, and the yarn seems to waltz about in the daylight glow. Today, she plans to give Johanna a birthday present that she has kept secret for months. It's a small lace collar, just like the one she is wearing herself... and it's one her friend admires very much.

Not too far away, in the kitchen, Johanna is busy, too. Today is Anna's birthday, and she's making her friend a breakfast fit for a queen: a pot of fresh milk with which she hand-fashions the finest of chocolates. Johanna molds them into a crown for the special occasion. All warm and round, the sweets glisten in the first rays of the sun.

It's a strange twist of fate: Anna, the daughter of the master of the house, was born on the same day as Johanna, the daughter of the housemaid. Is that why they became friends?

Mousse and lace: from the bottom of the pitcher and from the end of the spindles, a thin white mesh flows like a stream running towards the sea.

Through the cracked tile, the wind from the open sea pierces the room and comes to a standstill on the old chalk wall. Johanna shivers. One day, she will come to treasure the sea breeze. But now is not the time for dreams. Her friend awaits her. Basket in hand, she vanishes into the mist ascending from the canals.

— Happy Birthday!

— *Wel bedankt !*

Full of excitement, the girls exchange gifts with each other. The joy is written in their eyes. But there is something they were not expecting. The two friends discover an envelope under a large painting in the lounge.

It simply says: *'For your birthday'*.

— A letter? Voor ons? 'Well, what does it say?', exclaims Johanna, for whom the handwriting on the note remains a mystery. Anna carefully unwraps the mysterious letter and immediately recognizes her father's handwriting. Facing the window, she starts to read:

Dear children,

As I take up my pen this evening, it is to disclose something to you that has been kept a secret for so many years. It is something I can express far more easily in writing than I can with my own voice. You are now grown up and old enough to discover what really happened on October 12th, 1654.

On that day…

the sky over Delft was blue, and it was one of those beautiful autumn mornings when, little by little, under a shower of leaves, the canal water became streaked in gold and reddish-orange hues. Suddenly, toward ten o'clock in the sky, a thunderclap made the earth shake and a massive flash of light occurred: a powder keg had just exploded. The town was instantly covered by thick, black smoke. Braving danger, a young boy named Pieter hurried forward to help the injured. At the first house he approached, which belonged to Carel the painter, he heard a goldfinch twittering at the end of the courtyard. Fascinated, he moved closer, and in the ruins of the workshop under a crumbling wall, he discovered a basket.

It was a small crib! Carel's easel must have shielded it from the falling debris after the explosion. It looked as if the sea on the canvas Carel had been painting were a blanket that protected and covered the crib. Pieter hurriedly seized the wicker basket and whisked it far away from the commotion and flames.

He then ran lickety split to his sister, Monika, our long-beloved servant.
She would know how to look after the little survivor.

— 'Good heavens!', cried Monika as she uncovered the basket. When she
lifted the tiny blanket, she was dumbstruck. There was not just one
baby there, but two! Two little lace collars, so beautiful and both huddled
together. Monika had dreamt of having a child of her own for a long time.
But to feed two mouths would be too much for her humble means. So with
two white bonnets from which to choose, she closed her eyes and randomly
pulled one of the little ones up into her arms.

Monika then went to drop off the basket at our door.
An orphan child would always be taken in by our large family,
and she knew that. It was only shortly before she passed
away that our dear Monika confessed the truth to us. Long
before that, however, a beautiful friendship had been born.

The letter slips from Anna's hands. Facing the mirror, the two girls gape at each other. Life had both separated and formed them, each in her own manner. One became the daughter of the master of the house and the other the daughter of a maid. Anna had become as big and hearty as Johanna was slender and diminutive. Johanna's skin was tanned by the open air and chapped by the water buckets, while Anna's was smooth and pale. However, they both shared the same things that sisters often do: the same smile and the same favorite color.
For both of them loved the yellow of the sand and sun.
— 'You and I', says Anna.
— *'Jij en ik'*, whispers Johanna.
As they fall into each other's arms, the large painting in the salon, with its blend of velvety waves, seems to be watching them in contemplation.

And at the same time, the two sisters have an idea. While a thousand reflections are dancing on the rooftops of the town and on the hulls of the boats, 'bonnet white' and 'white bonnet' find themselves on the wharf where a river barge is moored. In a short while, it will be heading up the channel with the flow of the current.

One of the girls is wearing her little white collar, while the other dons a crown of wheat. Anna and Johanna advance hand in hand. Drops of light, grains of golden sand, blueish white waves... how beautiful is this place they have finally discovered! This unknown sea had once appeared on the top of a canvas – the canvas that had saved and cradled them both. Anna and Johanna stay where they are for quite a while just to admire the view. At last, they set down some bread rolls and chocolates on the beach and rush towards the dancing waves.

Jan Vermeer

The Milkmaid

c. 1658/60, oil on canvas, 45,5 x 41 cm, or 18 x 16 in
Rijksmuseum, Amsterdam, Netherlands
Photo: © Bridgeman - ARTOTHEK

The Lacemaker

1665, oil on canvas mounted on wood, 24 x 21 cm, or 9 ½ x 8 ¼ in
Musée du Louvre, Paris, France
Photo: © Peter Willi - ARTOTHEK

Jan Vermeer

13 South St.
Hanover, NH 03755
http://howelibrary.org

Who was Jan Vermeer ?

Little is known about this 17th century painter who was born in the small town of Delft in the Netherlands. His father was an innkeeper and traded in artwork. Jan (Johannes) Vermeer married in 1653 and had many children – at least 10! In the same year, he was admitted into the Guild of St. Luke as a master painter. Leaving his wife and children saddled with debt, he died in 1675 at the age of 43. All that remains of Vermeer are his paintings …

Was he famous?

Of course, Vermeer had patrons and sponsors who helped him with money. But because he didn't become famous in his lifetime, the world largely forgot about him until the 19th century. Then, in 1842, Étienne-Joseph-Théophile Thoré, an art critic and art historian, acknowledged Vermeer as one of the grand masters of Dutch painting. The small number of his paintings – around 35 – and the negligible amount known about his life only fueled an increased interest in the 'Sphinx of Delft'. Marcel Proust, the 20th century writer, was a great admirer of Vermeer and his *View of Delft* in particular, which he considered the 'most beautiful painting in the world' with its 'perfect little yellow wall'.

What makes a Vermeer painting so distinguishable?

Vermeer draws the viewer into a world where time seems to stand still, eternally capturing a moment of life's silence. His use of light and shade (a technique called chiaroscuro) to show the play of sunlight on a room, the subtle expressions on his characters' faces, the representation of day-to-day life in Dutch interiors – what we might call character scenes – all make up Vermeer's art. The painter used a lot of ultramarine blues from lapis powder, which was a very expensive pigment. This fits because blue was in many ways Delft's own color, given that all the enameled clay tiles and earthenware were painted in the very same shade.

What is known about *the lacemaker* and *the milkmaid*?

Nobody knows who the girls absorbed in their daily chores are. Vermeer immortalized them in two of his greatest paintings. While other artists choose to create portraits of noble and wealthy folk, Vermeer preferred anonymous models. With her head tilted over her hands, the lacemaker appears on a small canvas (24 x 21 cm, or 9 ½ x 8 ¼ in), forcing the viewer to focus on her actions. The painting's minute details are done with such close attention: just look at the lace collar. The milkmaid is a well known image today – advertising saw to that! Dressed in yellow and blue, silent and gazing downwards, she gently pours milk into a bowl. All is suspended for a brief moment as the objects shimmer in the light: the fabrics, earthenware, pewter, wicker work, skin, bread and milk…

Where can we see Jan Vermeer canvases?

Vermeer paintings can be seen at major museums around the world, including the Frick Collection in New York and the National Gallery in London. *The Lacemaker* resides at the Louvre Museum in Paris, as does *The Astronomer*. But the best place to see Vermeer's art is in his homeland: the Netherlands. At the Rijksmuseum in Amsterdam are: *The Milkmaid, The Woman in Blue Reading a Letter, The Love Letter* and *The Little Street*; while at the Mauritshaus in The Hague are *Girl with a Pearl Earring* and *View of Delft*.